MELANIE BROWN GOES TO SCHOOL

ff

MELANIE BROWN GOES TO SCHOOL

Pamela Oldfield

illustrated by Carolyn Dinan

faber and faber
LONDON · BOSTON

First published in 1970
by Faber and Faber Limited
3 Queen Square London WC1N 3AU
Faber Fanfares edition published in 1979
This edition first published in 1989
Reprinted 1989

Printed in Great Britain by
Cox & Wyman Ltd, Reading, Berkshire

A CIP record for this book is available from the British Library

ISBN 0–571–15346–1

Contents

for Carole and David

Melanie Brown and the Box of Straws

Melanie Brown had brown hair, and she wore it in two bunches. She was a naughty little girl, and she always had her own way. So when she reached the age of five and decided to go to school, that was that.

Her mother bought her a grey pleated skirt, a white blouse and a red jumper. There was also a grey blazer to wear over it. Melanie Brown put it all on and decided that it suited her, so that was no problem.

Grandmother gave her a new brown satchel, and on the 7th of September Melanie Brown went to school. She had quite made up her mind to like it, so she did.

She liked her teacher, whose name was Miss Bradley. She liked the big sunny classroom with the tables and chairs that were just the right size. She liked the sand-tray with the rubber buckets and spades. Also the Wendy House with the dolls and the cot and the pretend stove with its saucepans and kettle. She liked the big building bricks, the paints and crayons, the plasticine and the beads and many other things.

Then there were the stories. Miss Bradley was good at telling stories. She told the children stories about animals, stories about magic, stories about trains and buses, stories about children. There were sad stories and funny stories and stories about real things that happen in the world.

But although Melanie Brown enjoyed all these things there was one thing that she longed to do, and that was to give out the straws at milk-time. Every morning two boys from another class came in with a crateful of milk bottles. The teacher made a hole in each silver milk top and chose one child to give out the bottles, and another to give out the straws. Melanie Brown watched very carefully, and it looked quite simple.

So one morning, as soon as the big boys came in with the milk, she held her hand right up in the air, so that the teacher was sure to notice it.

'What is it, Melanie?' asked the teacher.

'Please, Miss Bradley, may I give out the straws?'

Miss Bradley looked at her doubtfully. Melanie Brown had only been at school for a few days.

'I think not today,' she said, 'but you may clean the blackboard if you like.'

Melanie Brown stared at her in amazement.

'Oh, but, Miss Bradley – I don't want to clean the blackboard,' she said firmly. 'I only want to give out the straws, because I'm *good* at giving out straws, but I'm *not* good at cleaning blackboards.'

Miss Bradley laughed.

'Oh, well. You can try, I suppose. Fetch the straws from the cupboard.'

Feeling very important, Melanie Brown went to the big cupboard where the straws were kept. She hoped that all the children were watching her. A boy called Jimmy was giving out the bottles.

Standing on tiptoe she took down the box and began to walk round. She looked in the box. Melanie Brown had never seen so many straws. She could not see all of each straw because they were standing up on end, packed closely together, but she could see the top of each one, like a tiny round hole. Suddenly she decided to count them.

'One, two, four, seven – ' she began, but she was not very good at counting.

She started again. 'One, two, three, seven, five, eight – ' No, that was not right.

Carefully, Melanie Brown began again, touching each straw as she said a number.

'One, two, three, eleven, eight, twenty – ' She was so busy counting that she had forgotten what she was supposed to be doing. The children watched her impatiently.

'Melanie, hurry up, dear,' said Miss Bradley. 'Christopher's table is waiting for straws.'

Melanie Brown frowned, and looked up.

'I'm trying to count them,' she said crossly, 'but the numbers keep going wrong.'

'Well, you must finish giving them out now, or else let Jennifer do it. It's nearly playtime.'

Melanie Brown suddenly remembered that she had meant to show everyone how quickly she could do the job. She darted forward towards Christopher's table, caught her elbow against the corner of Miss Bradley's desk and dropped the box. As it fell, the straws scat-

3

tered in all directions. Melanie Brown stared at them, where they lay, all white and new-looking. She thought there must be hundreds and hundreds of them. Or millions and millions.

The silence that followed was broken by Jennifer.

'Miss Bradley, Melanie Brown's dropped the straws!'

Melanie Brown looked slowly up at the teacher's face. She felt so terrible that she almost decided to give up school altogether.

But Miss Bradley only sighed.

'Never mind, Melanie, it was an accident. Perhaps Jennifer will help you to pick them up. We'll put them back in the box and use them for something else.'

And she sent Christopher into the next class for another box of straws and told him to finish giving them out. Melanie Brown was rather disappointed about that but Christopher was a very nice boy and he put two straws in her bottle, instead of only one. She looked at him carefully. He had fair hair and big blue eyes and such a nice smile that Melanie Brown decided to marry him when she grew up.

That afternoon Miss Bradley showed the children how to make shapes using the straws and some pipe-cleaners. She bent a pipe-cleaner in the middle and slipped a straw on to each half. That made a corner. Then she bent two more pipe-cleaners and fitted them into the straws. One more straw and it turned into a triangle. Then the children made some shapes. Melanie Brown made a square and Christopher made a shape with five sides, called a pentagon.

Melanie Brown thought he was the cleverest boy in the class. She was almost glad then that she had been chosen to give out the straws.

Melanie Brown and the
Pencil Sharpener

Melanie Brown liked school. She liked it the very first day, and every day she liked it a little bit more. She liked going into the hall, which was a big room with no desks in it. There was a piano at one end, and a stage at the other. Sometimes they went into the hall for singing and games, and Miss Bradley played the piano. They also went into the hall for prayers, with all the other classes.

Melanie Brown enjoyed it all so much that when Saturday came, and there was no school she was very disappointed. She was especially disappointed because she wanted to sharpen the pencils. The child who did that job was allowed to go into school early, so that the pencils would be ready for the others when they came in. Melanie Brown was quite sure that she would be good at sharpening pencils.

The reason was simple. Miss Bradley had a special pencil sharpener. It was made of shiny green metal, but you could look through a tiny plastic window to see what was happening inside. To sharpen a pencil you put it into a hole at one side of the sharpener, and turned a handle on the other side. Little shavings of wood came off the pencil and made the point sharp again.

Melanie Brown made up her mind to ask Miss Bradley if she could have the job on Monday, and she could hardly wait. But on Monday it was raining hard, and she wore her new black wellingtons and her mackintosh with the hood. The boots were made of rubber so Melanie Brown thought they ought to be bouncy, so she jumped over a puddle to see if they were. They were, so she tried to jump over a large puddle, but she landed right in the middle of it, and sat down with a great splash. When she got up again she was so wet she had to go home and change her clothes.

By the time she reached school the pencils were already sharpened. She was so disappointed that she could not do her work properly, and did some rather horrible writing patterns in her book. Miss Bradley gave red stars to the children who had tried hard, but she frowned at Melanie Brown's book, and did not give her a star.

Melanie Brown was surprised at how badly the day was going, but suddenly she had an idea. Miss Bradley had a special red pencil for marking the books. She would sharpen it and give Miss Bradley a surprise! She waited patiently until playtime, and went out into the playground with the other children. When Miss Bradley left the classroom to have her coffee, Melanie Brown went up to the teacher who was looking after them in the playground.

'Please, Mrs Jones,' she said, 'may I go into the classroom to fetch my hanky?'

It was rather naughty of her, because the hanky was in her pocket all the time.

Mrs Jones said 'Yes,' so she hurried inside. It was quiet in the classroom with all the children outside. She went straight to Miss Bradley's desk and looked for the red pencil. It was not on the desk, so she opened the drawer and there it was, next to the pen. It was a new pencil, very long, with gold writing along one side. Quickly she put it into the pencil sharpener, and began to turn the handle.

It made a lovely grinding noise. When she looked in through the plastic window, she saw little curly pieces of wood being shaved off the pencil. She began to turn the handle faster and faster, in case playtime ended before she had finished. As the handle went round the sound reminded her of a train going along. She slowed the handle down, to let the train stop at the station, then speeded it up again as it went on its journey.

When at last she took the pencil out it had a very sharp point, but it looked much smaller than before. Melanie Brown pressed it into the desk, and it made a tiny hole, but then the point snapped right off, so she had to start all over again. She looked through the plastic window, but there were so many curls of wood she could not see the pencil point. With a last burst of energy she sent the handle whizzing round. When her arm began to ache she stopped and drew out the pencil. She looked at it carefully. It was very short. So short, in fact, that all the gold writing had disappeared, and that made her wonder if something had gone wrong.

At that moment the whistle blew and playtime was over. Melanie Brown put the pencil back into the desk and ran outside to line up with the others. Nothing happened for a long time after that. Miss Bradley told them a story about Jack and the Beanstalk. Then they drew a picture about it, while one of the older girls read her reading book to Miss Bradley.

Then Miss Bradley looked in her desk for her long red pencil. When she found it she looked very puzzled indeed.

'Who has been playing about with my pencil?' she asked.

Most of the children looked up at her in surprise, but Melanie Brown went on drawing.

'Melanie Brown, have you done this?' said Miss Bradley, holding up the pencil. Everyone stared when they saw how small it was.

'Please, Miss Bradley, I wanted to sharpen it, and give you a surprise,' said Melanie Brown, in a voice that was almost as small as the pencil.

'Well, you have certainly given me a surprise, but not a very nice one,' said Miss Bradley. 'When did you do it?'

When Melanie Brown told her she was rather cross at first, but then she began to smile, and every time she looked at the pencil she smiled a bit more. Then, of course, all the children began to laugh – even Melanie Brown.

Miss Bradley said that luckily she had another red pencil, so they could all get on with their work, but she asked Melanie Brown not to give her any more surprises, and Melanie Brown said she would try.

Melanie Brown Cuts Out

Melanie Brown had brown hair, tied with ribbon in two bunches, one at each side of her head. When it was not tied in bunches, it hung down almost to her shoulders. She had always liked the bunches but not any more. Because Pat had long fair hair that hung down to her waist in twisty curls called ringlets. And that is what Melanie Brown wanted, only her ringlets would have to be brown.

So the next time Mrs Brown wanted to take her to the hairdresser, to have her hair trimmed, she made such a fuss that finally Mrs Brown said she could grow it. Every day Pat measured it for her with a tape-measure, and it was growing very nicely when something unfortunate happened.

One day Melanie Brown came in from the playground and found scissors and coloured paper on the desks. Miss Bradley showed the children how to fold the paper and make little snips round it. When she unfolded the paper, they were surprised to see that the holes had made a pattern. They all hurried back to their desks and started to make patterns of their own. Now Melanie Brown was not very good at cutting out. She made the snips too big and then cut the

paper in half by mistake. She tried again, but then the snips were too small, and when she unfolded the paper there was hardly any pattern.

But John's pattern was very good, and he pasted it on to a sheet of white paper. The white paper showed through the holes and looked very attractive. Pat's pattern was good, too, and she pasted hers on to black paper. Melanie Brown looked at her scissors to see what was the matter with them, but they looked just like all the other scissors. Miss Bradley gave her another piece of paper, and helped her to make a few snips. Then she tried again on her own, but when she opened it out all the snips had joined together into one big hole. Scowling, Melanie Brown screwed it up and dropped it on the floor under her desk. At once John put his hand up.

'Miss Bradley, Melanie Brown has thrown hers on the floor.'

But Miss Bradley did not hear him. Melanie Brown took Pat's scissors while she was not looking. John put his hand up again.

'Miss Bradley, Melanie Brown has taken Pat's scissors.'

Miss Bradley hurried over to them.

'All the scissors are the same,' she said. 'If you don't want to make a pattern, Melanie, why not make a picture instead – a house or a clown, perhaps.'

Pat leaned over the table.

'Shall I help you to make a pattern?' she asked kindly.

Melanie Brown's scowl deepened.

'I don't want to make a pattern,' she said, 'because I don't even like patterns. I'm going to make a house.'

She cut out a square for the house and a triangle for the roof. But the roof was too small for the top of the house, so she cut out a much bigger roof and pasted it on over the small one.

'Look at my house,' she said, in a pleased voice. John looked at it.

'It hasn't got any windows or any door.'

'I'm just going to make them,' said Melanie Brown crossly, and she cut out a little red door and four blue windows. When John saw it he liked it so much he decided to make a house, too. But Pat did not like it at all.

'The windows are bigger than the door,' she said, 'and the roof is too big.'

Angrily Melanie Brown poked her tongue out at her, and Pat pulled a horrible face back. Melanie Brown turned to John.

'I don't like houses,' she said in a loud voice. 'I'm going to make a clown.'

But even the clown went wrong, and then it was time to stop. Melanie Brown put her hand up at once.

'Please can I collect the scissors, Miss Bradley?'

'No, I'm afraid not, Melanie, it's Stephen's turn today.'

Melanie Brown sat back in her chair, swung her legs, and hated everything! She hated school; she hated cutting out; she hated Pat and John; and most of all she hated Stephen. She hated Stephen so much that when he came to collect her scissors she hid them in her desk, and pretended they were lost. There was no time to look for them because they had to go into the hall to watch a programme on the television. Melanie Brown did not enjoy it very much, because Pat was not her friend any more, and they did not sit together as they usually did.

When they went back to the classroom Miss Bradley chose six patterns to put up on the wall. One of them was Pat's and that made Melanie Brown so jealous she wanted to do something really bad to her. She took the scissors out of her desk, and cut the end off one of Pat's ringlets! Pat turned round quickly and saw the little curl on the floor. She snatched the scissors and made a big snip in Melanie Brown's hair. Melanie

Brown screamed, and tried to get the scissors back again, and then John joined in. They made such a noise Miss Bradley heard them.

She took the scissors away at once, and was very cross with both the girls. But when she found out just how naughty Melanie Brown had been she sent her to sit at an empty desk all by herself. She also wrote a note to each girl's mother to explain what had happened.

When Mrs Brown saw Melanie Brown's hair she said it would have to be trimmed, because one side was so much shorter than the other. Melanie Brown cried and cried when she heard that, but when she looked in the mirror she saw just how funny it looked, and started to laugh.

'Anyway,' she said defiantly. 'I don't like long hair any more,' and she blew her nose very loudly, and that was that!

Melanie Brown and the Dinner-Money

Monday was dinner-money day. A few of the children went home to dinner, but most of them had their dinner at school, in the big hall. So every Monday they took their dinner-money to school and Miss Bradley collected it. Some children, like Melanie Brown, took their money in a purse so that they would not lose it on the way to school. Some took it in an envelope, but one or two of them carried it in their hands.

One of these children was called Jimmy, and one Monday, while he was taking off his coat, he dropped his money on the floor. All the children were taking off their hats and coats and changing their shoes, so it was very difficult to see where the money went to. Jimmy searched for a few minutes and found what he could. Then he sat down in his place.

'Children with dinner-money come out, please,' said Miss Bradley, and she counted the money from each child and wrote it down in the dinner book. When it was Jimmy's turn she said, 'I think you've lost some of yours, Jimmy.' So he told her what had happened.

'You'd better have another look for it,' she said. 'Take someone to help you.'

So Jimmy chose Melanie Brown and together they

searched the cloakroom. They looked along the window-sill, under the shoe baskets, and even under the doormat, but it was no good. They could not find the missing money.

Then Jimmy said he might have dropped some of it in the playground before he came into school, so Miss Bradley sent them outside to look. They found a blue glove belonging to a girl in the top class, and took it in to her. They asked the top class if anyone had found any money, but no one had. Jimmy looked very miserable.

'My mother will be cross with me,' he said, 'when she knows I've lost my money.'

Melanie Brown felt sorry for him.

'Maybe you dropped it in the lane coming to school,' she suggested. 'Let's ask Miss Bradley if we can look in the lane.'

When they got back into the classroom it was time to go into the hall for prayers, but Miss Bradley said they could go afterwards.

All the other classes were in the hall with their teachers. Mrs Jones played some quiet music on the piano until the headmistress came in. Then they all said 'Good morning,' and sang a hymn called 'All things bright and beautiful' which was Melanie Brown's favourite. She did not know all the words, but she liked to hum the tune and listen to the older children. Then they put their hands together to help them think, and said a prayer about animals, and another one about people who were ill.

When they got back to the classroom Miss Bradley said they could go and look in the lane.

'But only for five minutes,' she told them, 'because it is nearly time for singing.'

The two children promised to be very quick, and off they went.

It was strange to be the only children out of school. It was quiet in the lane. Melanie Brown glanced back at the school. Denise and Christopher were watching them out of the window so she waved to them. Then she climbed up into the hedge and jumped down again, just for the fun of it. Jimmy tried it too, and they had a game to see who could jump the furthest. But then Jimmy slipped down and made his trousers all muddy, so they stopped that game and started to look for the money.

There was a field on one side of the lane, with a pond in it. The children collected ten stones each and they tossed them over the hedge into the pond, where they fell with a nice 'plopping' sound.

Then Jimmy found a small frog and tried to catch it, but the frog was a very good jumper, and at last he gave up in disgust.

'I like toads best,' he told Melanie Brown, 'because they don't keep jumping about all the time. Frogs are silly, aren't they?'

She agreed. Actually, she did not like toads or frogs, but she did not want to say so. By that time they had reached Mr Bloggs's cottage at the end of the lane. Mr Bloggs was the school caretaker. His fluffy black cat was sitting on the door-step in the sunshine, so they stroked it for a while. They tried to teach it to beg, but it was not very interested, and kept closing its eyes.

Then, with a rattle and a clatter, the milk van turned the corner into the lane. The children ran up to the milkman, both talking at once. He was surprised to see them there.

'Well, and what are you two up to?' he said.

They told him about the lost dinner-money.

'I'm afraid I can't help you there,' he said, 'but if you've finished looking for it, I'll take you back to school in the van.'

Eagerly they scrambled up into the front of the van and squashed up together on the small leather seat. It was a marvellous ride! The milkman whistled happily, the engine whirred, and the bottles shook and clinked together whenever they went over a bump in the road. It was all over much too soon. Melanie Brown wanted to make the adventure last a little longer, so she asked the milkman if they could help him to unload the bottles for the school.

'Well,' he said, 'I suppose you could. I'll do the big crates, and you can get the big bottles for the school kitchen.'

So they carried the big bottles from the van to the kitchen door, but just as Melanie Brown was carrying the last one, the milkman said, 'Oh, dear, here comes your headmistress.'

Melanie Brown took one look at the headmistress's face, and dropped the bottle. It smashed on the ground, and the milk spread out in a big white pool. 'What on earth are you two doing out here?' asked the headmistress. 'And who dropped that bottle?'

Just as the milkman was trying to explain Miss Bradley came out and *she* started to explain. The two children wisely said nothing at all, but when the explaining was over, they were in disgrace.

'I told you not to be more than five minutes,' Miss Bradley reminded them. 'You have missed the singing lesson.'

'But we were only looking for the dinner-money,' Jimmy protested, rather untruthfully.

'Susan found the money soon after you had gone,' said Miss Bradley, 'it was in her shoe. You have been naughty children and you will stay in at playtime.'

Jimmy was sorry, then, because he wanted to play football with his big brother at playtime. But not

Melanie Brown. She was not a bit sorry. It had been
such a marvellous adventure – she thought it was well
worth it!

Melanie Brown and the Cress

One morning Miss Bradley told them some exciting news. They were going to grow something in the classroom! Melanie Brown was very surprised, because there was no earth in the classroom. But Miss Bradley was talking about cress seeds. She showed them the picture on the seed packet, so that they would know what they were growing. When the cress had grown they could cut it and eat it.

'I'll bring some biscuits and butter,' she said, 'and it will be just like a picnic.'

They covered two large plates with white lint, and wetted it under the tap.

'Now,' said Miss Bradley, 'I'll give you each some seeds in your hand, and you can sprinkle them on to the plates. Try not to blow or cough on to the seeds, or they will be blown away.'

Melanie Brown waited breathlessly for her turn. The little brown seeds trickled out of the packet, into her outstretched hand. It felt so tickly she laughed. Yes, she laughed all over them, and away they flew. She stared at her empty hand. Miss Bradley sighed.

'Never mind, I'll give you some more.'

And out they trickled again, into her hand, and she

did *not* laugh. She carried them carefully to the plates, and let them fall on to the wet lint. Soon both plates were covered with a layer of tiny brown seeds.

'Now,' said Miss Bradley, 'we must take care of them. We'll leave them on the window-sill in the sunshine, and we'll water them every day, so they won't dry up.'

And they did. They took it in turns to water them, and every morning they hurried in to see how much the cress had grown overnight. But one day something went wrong with the cress, and this is how it happened. Melanie Brown was playing in the Wendy House, with Stephen, Denise, and Christopher. A Wendy House is a big play house, with a door that really opens and a window you can look through. Melanie Brown and Christopher were Mother and Father. Denise was the baby, and Stephen was the doctor. It was a good game. They dressed up in clothes from the dressing-up box, and the baby pretended to be ill.

The doctor looked at the baby's throat.

'The baby's got the measles,' he said. 'I'll go and get some special stuff to make her better.'

And he went out through the little door, to look for some pretend medicine. He saw the cress, and without stopping to think he pulled up a few stalks. When he gave them to the baby she was surprised, but she ate it all up. When the mother saw the baby eating the cress, she suddenly felt an attack of measles coming on. So did the father. The poor doctor had to fetch more and more cress.

Finally, of course, one plate of cress was empty, so they had to start on the other one. Then the doctor got the measles and he had to have some. All this time, Miss Bradley was busy with another group of children. She noticed how quietly the children were playing in the Wendy House, and she was pleased, because sometimes they argued about who was going to cook the dinner, and other important things.

When it was time to stop, the children put away the dressing-up clothes, and forgot about the game. But that afternoon Miss Bradley took some butter from her bag, and a packet of biscuits, so the children guessed what was going to happen. Miss Bradley chose three of them to butter the biscuits, and they all grew more and more excited. But the four naughty children grew more and more worried. They looked at each other and wondered what would happen when Miss Bradley found the empty plates.

Higher and higher grew the pile of buttered biscuits until at last they were all done. It was time to start the picnic! Miss Bradley sent Nicholas to fetch the cress, but all he found were the empty plates.

'It's gone,' he said, in a shocked voice. Everyone stared at him in astonishment. He showed them the two empty plates. Then Miss Bradley was really upset. She had planned such a lovely treat for them, and now it was spoilt. The children were so disappointed, they looked at each other in silent dismay.

'Someone very naughty has done this,' she said, 'and I want to know who it is.'

There was no answer. She looked slowly round the class. Suddenly Denise stood up, holding her tummy.

'Please, Miss Bradley, I feel sick,' she said.

Then Stephen stood up, too.

'I feel sick,' he said, and Miss Bradley looked at them in surprise. Reluctantly, Christopher stood up, and then Melanie Brown. Looking at their faces, Miss Bradley suddenly guessed *why* they were feeling sick.

'You four had better come out and tell me all about it,' she said.

They told her about the measles and the medicine, and as they did so, they began to realize how greedy and unkind it was, to leave nothing for the other children.

'You must tell the children how sorry you are,' said Miss Bradley. So they did.

'And I don't think you had better play in the Wendy House any more this week, because you might do something else naughty.'

The rest of the class ate the nice buttered biscuits, but there were none for the four naughty ones. Miss Bradley said they would grow some more cress another day, but somehow Melanie Brown was not very interested. She had had enough cress to last her for a long, long time!

Melanie Brown and the Green Shorts

Twice a week the children had a turn on the big apparatus. It was all set up in the hall for them and it was great fun. There were ladders and ropes, and a rope ladder. There were planks to slide down, and bars to swing on. All the children loved the big apparatus. Whenever they went on the big apparatus they wore shorts and T-shirts. Miss Bradley told them why.

'Your ordinary clothes would get in the way when you are climbing, and you might trip and fall. You would soon get too hot, too. Shorts and shirts are much more sensible.'

Melanie Brown understood this, but she did not like wearing hers. The reason was this. She was very vain, and she did not think they suited her. The shirt was white, but the shorts were green. Melanie Brown did not like green. One day she spoke to Miss Bradley about it.

'Please could I have some different shorts, because green doesn't suit me. Have you got any red ones?'

But Miss Bradley only laughed at the idea. 'Don't be silly, Melanie,' she said. 'Everyone else wears green without any fuss. The colour doesn't matter at all.'

But Melanie Brown thought differently, and

29

decided to do something about it. She would hide the shorts and pretend they were lost. But where could she hide them? There was nowhere in the classroom, but the door into the playground was open and that gave her an idea. Quickly she took her shorts and slipped outside. She looked around, and saw – a drainpipe. Without wasting a moment she pushed her shorts up into the pipe. When she was satisfied that they were out of sight she ran back into school, feeling very pleased with herself.

When it was time to change for the big apparatus Melanie Brown pretended to look for her shorts.

'Oh, Miss Bradley,' she said, in a surprised voice, 'I can't find my shorts.'

Miss Bradley had a look around.

'That's funny,' she said. 'Has anyone put Melanie's shorts on by mistake?'

Nobody had. She had another look, but of course she did not find them.

'Well, you can wear your knickers and vest just for today, Melanie.'

But Melanie Brown would *not*.

'Shall I ask my mother to buy me some red shorts?' she asked hopefully.

'Certainly not. We shall find them, sooner or later. Now if you won't wear your knickers and vest, you will have to sit and watch.'

So she did, and it was very boring. Christopher called out to her.

'Look at me – I'm upside down.'

Melanie Brown pulled a face at him, and would not

watch. Jennifer was hanging sideways on the bar, and Miss Bradley said she was a clever girl. Melanie Brown snorted loudly. 'Anyone can do that, it's easy,' she said. Nobody took any notice, however. They were enjoying themselves too much.

She sat and sulked until the lesson was over. Then Miss Bradley told them the story of Cinderella, and that made her forget all about the green shorts.

Later, while they were eating their dinner, it started to rain. Not just a shower, but a real downpour.

'It's a cloudburst,' said Christopher.

'I think it's a tropical storm,' said Nicholas, who had seen a tropical storm on the television.

They watched with interest as the rain lashed down. In no time at all the playground was full of big puddles. Suddenly, a lot of water began to overflow from the gutter. It poured down the window in a great sheet of water. The headmistress jumped up from the table.

'The gutter must be blocked,' she said. 'I'd better send for Mr Bloggs.'

Mr Bloggs, the caretaker, was a small, neat man. He always wore a dark blue boiler-suit. The children all believed he even went to bed in it. He arrived just as they were eating their apple pie. He was in a very bad mood. 'Messing about in all this rain – it's enough to give me my death of cold,' he grumbled. But he went off to the shed and came back with the ladder.

As soon as the children had finished their dinners, they hurried into the classroom to watch Mr Bloggs. He went up the ladder, carrying a long stick, in case he found what was blocking the gutter. Then he came down again, moved the ladder along a few yards, and went up again. He got wetter and wetter and his temper got worse and worse. But he found nothing. One of the big boys put his head out of the window.

'Mr Bloggs,' he shouted. 'Maybe there's a bird's nest in one of the drainpipes. That happened to us, once.'

Mr Bloggs was ready to try anything, so he went away to look in the drainpipes. Melanie Brown suddenly remembered her shorts! She ran to the door, but Miss Bradley called her.

'You can't go out in all this rain,' she said.

'But I've left something out there.'

'Well, it will have to stay there until the rain stops. Now find a comic to read.'

Melanie Brown found a comic, but she did not read it. She watched out of the window for Mr Bloggs. He went past, at last, carrying a very wet pair of green shorts. Melanie Brown remembered that her name was in the shorts. So they would soon know who had blocked up the drainpipe, and made the gutter overflow!

Later that afternoon, when the rain had stopped, the headmistress came in. She had Melanie Brown's shorts in her hand, and she spoke to Miss Bradley. Melanie Brown had to tell them how the shorts came to be in the drainpipe. They were both very annoyed. Then the headmistress took Melanie Brown along to see Mr Bloggs, and to tell him she was sorry.

'I didn't mean to cause you all that bother,' she told him.

'Well, see it doesn't happen again,' he said, and she promised.

Next time they went on the big apparatus, Melanie Brown was the first one to get changed.

'Do you know,' she said to Denise, 'I've changed my mind about green. I think it does suit me, after all!'

Melanie Brown and the Christmas Concert

As soon as Melanie Brown knew that there was going to be a Christmas concert she made up her mind she would be in it. Miss Bradley told them every class would be in the concert and all the mothers and fathers could come and watch. Melanie Brown was so excited she jumped up from her chair.

'Miss Bradley, I can sing. I'm good at singing. Can I be in the concert?'

'Sit down, Melanie,' said Miss Bradley, smiling. 'I haven't finished telling you about it yet.'

But Melanie Brown would *not* sit down.

'I can dance, Miss Bradley,' she said. 'Can I dance in the concert?'

'I've told you to sit down, Melanie. No one else is calling out. Please wait until I've finished.'

Melanie Brown sat down, but then jumped up again.

'I know, Miss Bradley. I can say a nursery rhyme. I can say Jack and Jill – '

'Melanie Brown!' said Miss Bradley, in a very cross voice. 'If you don't sit down and be quiet, you won't be in the concert at all!'

The children looked at Melanie Brown and she went

very red. She sat down as quickly as she could and tried to listen quietly while Miss Bradley told them about the concert.

She told them that the top class was going to sing some songs, the middle class was going to do some dances and their class was going to act a nativity play.

'A nativity play tells the story of the first Christmas and the birth of baby Jesus in the stable,' said Miss Bradley. 'We will act the story and sing some carols. Some of you will be dressed up as certain people in the story. Others will help with the singing.'

Then she began to choose the children for the different parts.

'Please, Miss Bradley, can I be Jesus?' asked Melanie Brown.

'No, dear. No one is going to be Jesus because Jesus is only a tiny baby in this play. Now be quiet, please.'

Denise was chosen to be Mary and Nicholas to be Joseph. Three boys would be the shepherds and another three the wise men. A few girls would be angels and the rest of the class would sing carols.

'Please, Miss Bradley, can I be the ox?' Melanie Brown asked hopefully. 'I can moo like an ox.'

'We aren't having any animals in it, dear. You are going to sing carols.'

'But Miss Bradley, I can't sing, but I *can* moo.'

'Stop being silly, Melanie. You told us just a moment ago that you were good at singing.'

Melanie Brown gave up. She sat in her chair with a very grumpy face while Miss Bradley told each of the children what to say, where to sit or stand, and when to move from one place to another. In spite of herself, she had to admit it sounded very exciting. In fact, it was the most interesting thing that had happened since she started school. She soon forgot her disappointment at not being an ox, and as the days went by she tried really hard, until she was the first to remember every word of the carols. Miss Bradley was very pleased with her.

But then something happened to make Melanie Brown naughty again. One day Miss Bradley brought a big cardboard box into the room and began to take out the clothes the children were going to wear.

Denise was to be Mary, so she wore a long blue

gown, with a white shawl over her head. Nicholas was to be Joseph and he wore a long green robe tied with a silk cord.

The shepherds were given ragged tunics and the angels long white gowns, but the wise men had velvet cloaks and crowns. It was the crowns that made Melanie Brown feel naughty again.

The crowns were made of cardboard covered with silver paper, decorated with jewels made from wine gums. Red wine gums were rubies and green wine gums were emeralds. The children gasped with delight when they saw the crowns, and Melanie Brown gasped louder than anyone else. She badly wanted to be a wise man so that she could wear one. She got up from her chair and went out to Miss Bradley.

'Miss Bradley, I don't want to be an ox any more,' she said firmly.

'No, dear, I know you don't.'

'I want to be a wise man.'

'Well, you can't be a wise man, Melanie, because you're a girl, and anyway you're a singer.'

'But I want to wear a crown.'

Miss Bradley reached into the box and pulled out some silver bands.

'Look,' she said, 'silver head-bands are for the singers. Try one on, Melanie. I'm sure it will look very nice on you.'

Melanie Brown took the silver head-band and walked over to the mirror. She banged it on her head and pulled a horrible face at herself in the mirror. The other singers put their head-bands on and they really

did look charming. Even Melanie Brown thought so, but she did not want to admit it. However, she kept the head-band on and went into the hall with the others to rehearse the play on the stage. It was fun.

Melanie Brown was longing for the day of the concert because her mother and father were coming and she wanted them to see her on the stage. Then they would see how grown-up she was now she was a schoolgirl.

The day of the concert came at last. Melanie Brown thought the morning would never pass and she was so excited she could hardly eat her dinner.

When it was time to start dressing up Melanie Brown's legs began to feel like jelly. She was glad she did not have any words to say, because she was so nervous she felt sure she would have forgotten them.

Miss Bradley was busy helping the children to get ready, but suddenly she glanced out of the window.

'Shh!' she said to the children. 'Look outside! The mothers and fathers are arriving. You must all be much quieter.'

Melanie Brown was standing next to Christopher, watching for their mothers and fathers to arrive. Christopher was a kind little boy and he said, 'Shall we change over for a little while? You can wear my crown and I'll wear your head-band.'

Of course, Melanie Brown was only too pleased, and before she knew what was happening she was in front of the mirror with the beautiful silver crown on her head. The longer she looked at herself the more certain she was that the crown looked better on her than it did on Christopher. If *only* she could have been a wise man! She suddenly felt angry with Miss Bradley, and jealous of Christopher, and she did a very naughty thing. She pulled off one of the red wine gums and put it in her mouth. It tasted rather odd, but she thought that must be the glue that Miss Bradley had used to stick it on. Then she ate one of the green wine gums, then another red one, and another green one, until they had all gone.

At that moment she heard Miss Bradley's voice.

'Christopher, where's your crown? Put it on quickly. It's nearly time to go into the hall.'

Melanie Brown snatched off the crown, and Christopher picked it up. He stared, and his eyes filled with tears.

Miss Bradley hurried over to them.

'Come along, get into line you two. Why, whatever is the matter, Christopher?'

When she saw the crown she was very angry, but there was no time to say anything just then. She was too busy trying to console Christopher. It would never do for one of the three wise men to be crying when he went to find Jesus.

'Cheer up, Christopher,' she said, drying his tears with a paper handkerchief. 'I think I've got some Smarties in the sweet tin. I'll stick some of those on the crown. They will look just as pretty.'

And sure enough, they did.

Then it was time for the nativity play, which was a great success. When it was all over the mothers and fathers clapped their hands for a long time, they had enjoyed it so much.

That evening, when Melanie Brown was eating her supper, her mother said, 'You sang beautifully in the concert, Melanie, but why weren't you wearing a silver head-band like the other singers?'

And, do you know, Melanie Brown had been so upset after spoiling Christopher's crown that she had forgotten to put her head-band on again. It made her sad, just to think about it.

But I think it was her own fault, don't you?

Melanie Brown and the Dentist

Melanie Brown always made a dreadful fuss when her mother took her to the dentist. I don't know why, but she did. The dentist was a friendly man, who smiled and joked with her, but still she did not like him. She did not even like the chair that tipped up and down. And she always made a fuss. She kicked and cried and screamed. The poor man could never persuade her to open her mouth, not even a tiny bit, so no one knew whether any of her teeth needed mending.

So when Miss Bradley told them one morning that the school dentist was coming to look at their teeth, Melanie Brown did not know what to do. She looked round to see if the other children would make a fuss.

Susan was clipping a sheet of paper on to the painting easel, Christopher was rolling up his sleeves by the sand-tray, and Denise was softening a large lump of plasticine. No one seemed to be worrying about the dentist.

She went over to the Wendy House, and looked in. Nicholas was there, pulling a white coat from the dressing-up box. He looked up.

'Do you want to play?' he asked.

'What are you playing – doctors?'

'No, dentists. I'm the dentist. You can be the mother if you like and the doll can be your little girl.'

'I don't want to play dentists,' said Melanie Brown crossly. 'It's a silly game.'

'All right, don't play,' said Nicholas. 'I'll ask Paula.'

Melanie Brown sat down on a chair, put her thumb in her mouth, and watched him crossly. Paula, it seemed, *wanted* to play 'dentists' and they both disappeared inside the Wendy House.

Melanie Brown began to swing her legs, kicking the leg of the desk.

She thought it was very mean of Paula to play with Nicholas. She jumped up and looked in at the window of the Wendy House.

'I'm going to play with the farm, Paula,' she told her. 'Do you want to play with me?'

'No, thank you,' said Paula politely. 'I want to play "dentists".'

Melanie Brown was so annoyed that she poked her tongue out at them and went back to her chair. No one took any notice of her so she began to kick the leg of the desk again, as hard as she could. Miss Bradley heard her and looked up.

'Don't make that noise, Melanie Brown,' she said sharply. 'Find something to do.'

So she wandered over to the sand-tray where Christopher was making tunnels in the sand.

'These tunnels are caves,' he said. 'I'm pretending the sea comes in and fills them with water. Do you want to play?'

'Tunnels are stupid,' said Melanie Brown, and she

44

reached into the sand-tray and pushed in the tunnels. She thought Christopher would start to cry but he did not. He hit her on the hand instead, with the rubber spade. Melanie Brown screamed and began to cry. She cried as loudly as she could because she did not want

Miss Bradley to hear Christopher when he told her about the tunnels. But Miss Bradley did manage to hear and she said, 'Stop crying, you naughty girl. It was your own fault. What is the matter with you this morning? You're not usually so silly.'

And she gave her a book and a pencil and some tracing-paper. But Melanie Brown did not want to trace a picture, so she poked the pencil through the paper and made a hole in it. Then she scribbled on the back of the chair and dropped the pencil down the back of the cupboard. She was determined to be a real nuisance.

Just then, however, the classroom door opened and a lady came in. She was the prettiest lady Melanie Brown had ever seen. She had brown eyes and black hair which curled softly all over her head, and she wore a necklace of pink and white beads. Her dress was pink and her shoes were white with tiny white bows. Melanie Brown decided that as soon as she was grown-up she would look like that.

The lady talked to Miss Bradley and they both laughed a lot.

Then the lady looked at her watch and said, 'Well, give me ten minutes and then send the first six in,' and went out again.

Melanie Brown took a sheet of paper from the table and found her crayons. She began to draw a princess with short black curls and a pink dress and white shoes.

She was still busy drawing when Miss Bradley called her out to the front, with Stephen and Susan and three other children. They went through the hall and into the room where the teachers had their coffee. There, to Melanie Brown's surprise, was the pretty lady, wearing a white coat and holding a bundle of cards. Miss Bradley told the lady the children's names and each child was given her own card. The pretty lady was the dentist!

Melanie Brown was first. She sat on a chair and opened her mouth and the lady looked at all her teeth with a little mirror on a stick.

'What nice teeth,' said the lady, smiling. 'Do you clean them every morning and every night?'

Melanie Brown nodded shyly.

'Good girl. Next one, please,' said the dentist, and that was all. It was almost disappointing. Melanie Brown began to wonder why she had always made such a fuss.

When she got back to the classroom she finished her picture of the princess and put it in her coat pocket to show her mother. Then she ran over to the Wendy House and asked Nicholas if she could play 'dentists'.

Melanie Brown and the Sugar Mice

One morning the children went into the hall, and saw a big, big Christmas tree. It was the biggest Christmas tree that Melanie Brown had ever seen. It stood in one corner and it was so wide it touched the walls with its branches. It was so high that it nearly touched the ceiling. The roots were planted in a big red pot, and beside the tub was a box full of decorations. Melanie Brown was so excited that she forgot the words of the hymn. She turned round so many times to look at it that the headmistress told her to pay attention.

Later that morning Miss Bradley told them that they were going to have a Christmas Party.

'We will have games and a party tea,' she said, 'and then one of Father Christmas's fairies will give every child a present. There will be a small present on the tree, too, for you to take home to your brothers and sisters.'

All the children clapped with delight – all except Melanie Brown, that is. She felt cheated because she did not have any brothers or sisters. Jennifer had a baby brother, and Christopher had two sisters. The more she thought about it, the more she decided it was not fair. So she made herself look as miserable as possible, and waited for Miss Bradley to notice her.

'What's the matter, Melanie?' said Miss Bradley at last. 'Don't you like parties?'

Melanie Brown tried to squeeze out a few tears but they would not come.

'It's not fair,' she said. 'I haven't got any sisters or brothers, so I won't have a present off the tree.'

'But you will have a big present from the fairy,' said Miss Bradley patiently, 'and the presents on the tree will only be small presents.'

Jennifer asked her what the small presents would be.

'Sugar mice, I think,' she said. 'Now, that's enough about the party. We must do some work.'

That night, as she lay in bed, Melanie Brown thought about the sugar mice, and the more she thought about them the more determined she became to get one, somehow. So the next day, when it was news-time, Melanie Brown stood up. 'My Mummy is having a baby,' she said.

'Is she?' said Miss Bradley, surprised. 'It will be nice for you to have someone to play with, won't it? When is the baby coming?'

'The day of the party,' said Melanie Brown, 'so may I have a sugar mouse?'

'Melanie Brown!' laughed Miss Bradley. 'You are making all that up, just so that you can have a sugar mouse. What a greedy girl!'

So that was no good. But the next morning, as luck would have it, Melanie Brown found herself right next

to the Christmas tree at prayer-time. When everyone
closed their eyes for the prayer, she kept hers open.
Slowly she reached up and her fingers closed round a
little pink mouse. With a quick tug she tried to pull
it down, but – oh dear! The mouse was tied on too

tightly. The branch shook, and all the silver balls
danced about. The headmistress heard them rustling
and opened her eyes, to see what was going on. Quick
as a flash Melanie Brown closed her eyes again. So
that was no good, either.

But Melanie Brown was a very determined little
girl, and she had made up her mind to have a mouse.
After prayers, Miss Bradley marked the register, and
asked her to take it to the headmistress. On the way
back Melanie Brown looked into the hall. There was
no one there. She ran straight to the tree, stood on
tiptoe, and bit the head off a yellow mouse. It was

delicious! She bit the head off a white mouse, and that was delicious, too. So was the pink mouse's head. They were so good that before she knew what she was doing, she had bitten off *all* the heads.

Then she ate a whole mouse and that was a bad mistake, because she forgot about the string tail. As she swallowed it, it stuck in her throat. She thought she was going to choke. She was coughing and spluttering when Mrs Jones came into the hall, and saw the poor little headless mice. She was very angry. She gave Melanie Brown a pat on the back, to make her cough up the string, and then took her to the headmistress.

'Melanie Brown, I'm surprised at you,' said the headmistress. 'You are a naughty, greedy girl. You do not deserve to go to the party, so you will go home instead.'

And that is what happened. Melanie Brown never did like sugar mice, after that.

Melanie Brown and the Policemen

Melanie Brown woke up one morning. She felt sure something exciting was going to happen, but she could not remember what it was. She washed, dressed and ate her breakfast so quickly that she had a few moments to spare, and her mother said she could play in the garden with her ball. Because she was so excited, she bounced her ball very hard and it bounced right over the gate and into the road. Melanie Brown rushed after it. She didn't stop to see if there was any traffic coming, but ran straight into the road. HONK! HONK! HONK! Car brakes squealed as a large black car pulled up close beside her. A man leaned out of the window and shouted angrily at her.

'Lucky for you I've got good brakes, or you might have been run over. Don't you know you should never run into the road?'

Melanie Brown hung her head and didn't answer.

'Just you remember in future, young lady,' said the driver, and he drove away down the road.

Poor Melanie Brown was very upset. She picked up the ball and took it back indoors.

She was still very quiet when she arrived at school, and Miss Bradley wondered what was the matter, and

asked her if she felt ill. Melanie Brown shook her head.

'Well, cheer up then, dear. The policemen are coming today to give us a demonstration on road safety. Have you forgotten?'

So *that* was the exciting thing she had been trying to remember!

When it was time for the demonstration they all went into the big hall, and sat in rows, leaving a big space down the middle. There were three policemen in dark blue uniforms, with shiny silver buttons, and black shiny shoes. They did look tall. Melanie Brown felt very small and she sat very still.

Then one of the policemen talked to them about crossing the road, and he told them to pretend that the space in the middle of the hall was the road. He told two girls to walk up and down and pretend that they were going for a walk.

'They are quite safe,' he said, 'because the road is empty. There is no traffic at the moment. But look – whatever is this coming in?'

He pointed to the hall door and to everyone's amazement they saw a *car* coming in. A real car was coming in through the hall door! It was not a big car, of course, with an engine to drive it along, but it was quite big and it had pedals. It was bright red, with shiny silver bumpers and a black steering wheel. It had two headlamps and the seats were made of red leather. The policeman said he was going to choose someone to drive it! Someone who was sitting up nice and straight! Melanie Brown sat up *very* straight, but so did everyone else, and the policeman chose a boy called Simon. They all watched him climb into the car and thought him the luckiest boy in the school.

Then the two girls pretended to walk in the road again. Simon pedalled very hard and the car went along and bumped into one of the girls. She fell over and pretended she was hurt.

'Oh dear,' said the policeman. 'There's been an accident. I wonder why that happened. Does anyone know?'

Melanie Brown's hand went up straight away, so the policeman asked her to tell him.

'They were walking in the road,' said Melanie Brown, 'and not looking where they were going.'

'Good girl,' said the policeman.

Next, the policeman unrolled a big carpet. At least, it looked like a carpet when it was rolled up, but when it was unrolled it was striped in black and white. It was a pretend zebra-crossing. They laid it on the floor across the road, and the policeman brought in another car! This one was blue and silver with brown leather seats.

'Now, come along, little girl,' said the policeman to Melanie Brown. 'You were quick with your answer just now, so you can drive the blue car for us.'

Melanie Brown stood up and walked over to the car in a sort of dream. She sat on the brown leather seat and her feet just reached to the pedals in the bottom of the car.

Then they pretended that three children wanted to cross the road and the two cars had to drive along and stop to let them walk over the zebra-crossing. It was great fun pedalling along, just like a lady in a real car.

Denise was chosen next, to be a 'school-crossing lady'.

She dressed up in a white coat and carried a pole with a notice on the top which said 'STOP – CHILDREN CROSSING'. When the drivers saw the notice they had to stop while the children crossed the road.

Lastly they wheeled in a small ice-cream van and chose Christopher to be the driver. The policeman told them never to run across the road to an ice-cream van. Then he said, 'Keep looking both ways, and if it's safe walk across the road.'

The children promised to remember, and at last it

was over. The children were sorry to say 'good-bye' to the friendly policemen.

That afternoon, Miss Bradley told them there would be a prize for the best painting about road safety.

Melanie Brown painted a very big blue car and a

little girl waiting to cross the road. There was a very fat school-crossing lady in the picture, too, and squashed up very small in one corner there was an ice-cream van.

The headmistress thought it was the best and she gave Melanie Brown the prize. It was a small shiny blue torch, the same colour as the car!